A Very Special Lamb...

Goes Places

(Book 1)

A Very Special Lamb...
Goes Places

Written by Sharda Norman
Illustrated by Janelle Baker

GOD'S LAMBS
TRUST
He Gathers His Lambs in His Arms

To my precious children,
Hannah and Jonathon-James.

I thank God for you both; you are special and
have so much potential.

May you accomplish your purpose and fulfil your
destiny.

Acknowledgements

I would like to take this opportunity to say a HUGE thank you to all those who have helped me on this journey of success. Thank you to my family and friends who were supportive in seeing this book become a reality.

And now, a HUGE shout out and a MASSIVE THANK YOU to God Almighty that through His Son Jesus Christ of Nazareth, and the POWER of the Holy Spirit I am where I am today.

Foreword By Pastor Rick Johnston

Sharda has written this great children's book that can be read to them... or if they are old enough, they can read it aloud themselves. Children will connect with the story of a little lamb that is simply looking for life to be good and fun. The honest picture of joy, sorrow, loss and gain is a realistic picture for children to absorb. The life lessons and the questions for the child to answer are practical and helpful in developing both the understanding and reasoning facility of children. The story of life on the farm with other animals and the lamb's interaction with them is both humorous as well as instructive. Each child will have opportunity to see how this "Very Special Lamb" relates to them. This book will, no doubt, prompt a lot of discussion between parent and child across a whole range of issues.

From The Author To You

My name is Sarah. I have always believed that I am special, and you should believe that too!

Growing up, we were a flock of four with a daddy sheep, mummy sheep and two younger lambs; I was the oldest of the lambs.

I am so glad that you can come along with me, as I relive my life and share with you some of the things that I've been through on my journey. My experience was not a very happy one at times, but there have been some joyful memories along the way which I would like to share with you little lambs... Come with me on my journey and see what happened as I walked through life as **A Very Special Lamb.**

Chapter 1

As I sit here thinking and writing about myself as a lamb, it amazes me of how far I have come. I am very grateful to God for His help and saving mercies.

My first memories are of living near a flock of sheep that were very pleasant to me; they were kind and liked me very much. We would spend days playing with those sheep (that is, myself and my baby brother called Jimmy the Lamb). We would eat at their farm, they cared for us and spending time with them was fun. We were treated really special and enjoyed the kindness and love that was shown towards to us.

My own mummy sheep was also loving and fun to be with, she would cook and tidy up after us. She was a good homemaker; our home always looked clean and tidy. Daddy Sheep, on the other hand, went to work every day, and in his spare time he would join his friends to play cricket which he liked very much. In fact, he loved playing this game with other sheep.

Also, when we were invited out on special occasions, Daddy Sheep would dance. He was a *brilliant dancer* and other sheep and lambs would always stop to admire him. I thought he was amazing too and was proud that he was **my** daddy sheep. When other sheep and lambs were talking about his talent, this made me feel really good.

I remember us dancing at weddings, just the two of us on the dance floor. It was special for me, and I enjoyed that lamb and daddy sheep moment (*while learning to dance at the same time!*). He was such a graceful dancer and would seem completely lost in his dancing world. You could say that he loved dancing; you could always see the joy on his face. When he danced, he looked as though he was alone and like he was the only person in the room; his face shone with contentment and a sense of joy; he was having a great time. He truly enjoyed himself at parties, and lambs and sheep enjoyed watching him perform. I danced with him on many special occasions and it was great, but *he* was the star. He always put on a show and I was his number 1 fan.

Mummy Sheep was very caring and wanted us to be clean and tidy, but that didn't really work out most of the time because I was a messy lamb at times. However, Mummy Sheep was still willing to help us get cleaned up. She did a lot around the farm and it was hard with two little lambs and a daddy sheep. I appreciate all she did for us, and *oooooh* her cooking was always delicious! Anyone could come to our farm and get something to eat.

As time went by, I found out that the good thing about being a lamb was that we could do lots of fun things and have an enjoyable time with the grown-up sheep we felt safe with.

One day, in particular, I remember clearly when Daddy Sheep took us out to play with a remote-control boat that he had bought for us. There was a river near to our farm and lots of big boats would go by, so having a little boat of our own to play with was exciting.

We discovered, not far from our farm, a pond which was big enough for our boat to move around freely. So, Daddy Sheep took Jimmy the Lamb and I to the pond to play with our boat.

When Daddy Sheep placed the boat in the pond, we got very excited! It was difficult to get us lambs to stand still with so much excitement. We watched the boat go around, and around, and around, which made us both happy. We were having a great time with Daddy Sheep and our little boat.

It was always lovely to do fun things with Daddy Sheep. All lambs like spending time with their daddy sheep I am sure. I think we usually spend more time with our mummy sheep than with our daddy sheep, so having those precious moments with your daddy sheep, doing fun things, is really special (and should not be taken lightly). These special moments are especially good for building bonds between a daddy sheep and his lambs.

So, going out with Daddy Sheep was fantastic for Jimmy and me, and I have kept these memories in my heart to this very day. I was hoping we would get to do that again soon, but we never did.

What good memories do you have?
You can write them in the box below.

Chapter 2

I was a creative lamb that could find things to do to entertain myself, and I knew exactly how to do that. This sometimes got me into trouble with Mummy Sheep; she would make sure that I was always supervised, but this was sometimes very difficult because Mummy Sheep had another lamb to keep an eye on. I didn't like to sit still for a long time which was a challenge for her; getting myself busy was what I liked. I think I was very adventurous as a lamb.

This was something I liked doing: I would use my bed as a boat, Mummy and Daddy Sheep's bed as the port and the kitchen cupboards as the shop. This caused Mummy Sheep to get really upset with me on many occasions. She would sometimes find her groceries in my cot. She was not always happy with my creative ideas, she told me many times, but when you need to go shopping - you just have to do it!

Whilst I liked using my cot as a boat and my play pen, Mummy Sheep had another idea, she put Baby Lamb in it for his morning or afternoon nap. Now this was a very, very bad idea!!!!!

What??!!! Noooo, not my cot!

I didn't really like this new idea, even though it was explained to me. I wasn't interested in hearing what Mummy Sheep had to say about the changes that would happen. The truth of the matter was, I did not want any lamb sleeping in *MY* cot and I told Mummy Sheep this. You see, I didn't understand the reason why Baby Lamb had to sleep when I wanted to play in my cot. I refused to have him sleep in my cot, he did not realise what he was doing to my little life.

"Baby lambs need their afternoon naps," said Mummy Sheep.

"BUT NOT IN MY COT," I said.

After a while, I "agreed" for Baby Lamb to sleep in my cot. Mummy Sheep explained the situation at the farm, and she talked to me about the changes that would take place. She understood that I liked my cot, but we had to share sometimes as a flock.

So, I did agree, but I still wasn't happy. Baby Lamb had been sleeping in my cot for a while now, and this had been happening every day; I was frustrated with this new arrangement. This was not fair! Something needed to change, but what could I do? I decided to come up with a plan, and this is my plan...

While he was sleeping, I would grab his toes from the side of the cot and bite them. *Oooooh, that must have hurt... ouch!!!!*

When I would bite his toes, Baby Lamb would scream, and Mummy Sheep would come running to check on him. You must understand (and don't forget) that he was in my boat and I didn't like it one bit! Besides, the cot was mine. When he would cry out, poor Mummy Sheep would come running franticly to see what the problem was.

"Oh, little one, don't cry," she would say to comfort him.

This went on for a while, and she didn't realise that I was responsible for Baby Lamb's outbursts.

I got away with biting Baby Lamb's toes for a while, until one-day Mummy Sheep was getting him ready for his bath. She would normally give him a bath before he had a nap, but this particular day she washed him *after* his nap, and when she took off his socks, she noticed that he had teeth marks on his toes! Mummy Sheep was shocked as she wasn't sure 'who' or 'what' did it; *it could have been a mouse, but those were human teeth marks! Maybe it was a ghost!?*

She was shocked; it definitely alarmed her. She looked at me and said, "Sarah did you bite Baby Lamb's toes?"

I said "no" at first. Then she asked again.

"Sarah Meray, did you bite your little baby lamb's toes?"

I said, "yes, I did it."

Let's say Mummy Sheep was not impressed with me. She told me off for biting Baby Jimmy and then I had to say sorry to him. When I saw what I had actually done, I felt sorry for him too. I gave him a big hug and said, "sorry."

From that day Mummy Sheep had to keep a closer eye on me, but my argument still remained the same, "Why is he still sleeping in my boat and how am I going to play??!!"

Have you ever gone through a frustrating situation? How did you deal with it?

Chapter 3

After living at this farm for a while, Mummy Sheep told me that we would be leaving our farm and would be moving to Grandma and Grandpa Sheep's farm. Now this was a surprise to me. You see, we were living near to a flock that loved Baby Lamb and I; how would I live without this flock that loved us? In my little mind I couldn't see how this could be possible. I would miss them, and they would miss me too.

"I don't want to go, Mummy Sheep, can we please stay here?" I said. She knew I didn't want to leave and live on another farm.

"But we have to go," she said.

"Why are we leaving our farm, can we not stay, Mummy Sheep?" I asked her. "Oooh, but we love living here," I said.

This news made Baby Lamb and I really sad. We were going to miss the lovely sheep and they were going to miss us too. I wasn't sure if they would even remember us.

I later found out that the reason for leaving our farm, was that Daddy Sheep sold our farm with us inside and now we had to leave. This was upsetting to hear that our own Daddy Sheep would do something like this to us - *his little lambs.*

Mummy Sheep explained to me that we were going to live with Grandma and Grandpa Sheep on their farm for a little while. I had never been to visit their farm before, so I was not sure I'd like it there.

Mummy Sheep realising that I was uncertain

about our move, began to share with me all the exciting things that happened at Grandma and Grandpa Sheep's farm, but I was still not convinced that our move was a good idea.

"Will I remember my lovely flock when I leave and when will I be seeing them again?" I said to Mummy Sheep.

She could see that I was not happy to leave, and said, "Don't be sad, Little Lamb, there will be lots of things to entertain you at Grandma and Grandpa Sheep's farm."

She told me, "They have goats, cows, chickens, ducks and a dog; also, the farm is really, really BIG and you can play all day with your cousin lambs, you will love it there, my dear. You will get to go and pick fresh vegetables and fruits to eat. And not forgetting, you'll have lots of lambs to play with!"

I began to get really excited about our move to

Grandma and Grandpa Sheep's farm. After Mummy Sheep shared with me all the exciting things that were there for us to enjoy, I then began thinking about how amazing it might be to live on a BIG farm. Having new things to do there would distract me from thinking of the flock I'd leave behind at our old home. It was sad to think that our farm had so quickly become "our old farm." *Would I remember the wonderful times we had here?* I was not sure...

As days went by, the idea of leaving made me feel happy yet sad that we'd be leaving to go somewhere far away. Even though I wasn't certain about our move, I was beginning to feel rather excited about going to Grandma and Grandpa Sheep's farm where I would see the animals, play in the huge meadow and run around in the farm with my cousins. Also, not forgetting, meeting another flock of lambs and sheep for the first time.

Leading up to the move, I kept asking Mummy

Sheep, "When are we going to Grandma and Grandpa Sheep's farm?"

Every day, once or twice I'd ask, or sometimes more, "When are we going to Grandma and Grandpa Sheep's farm?"

AGAIN, AND AGAIN, I would ask, "When are we going to Grandma and Grandpa's Sheep farm?"

Mummy Sheep was not pleased that I was asking her so often, but I just wanted to know. It seemed as though everything was taking a very long time to become a reality. Have you ever wanted something so much and felt as though it was taking too long to come to you? Well, this is exactly how I was feeling. I just couldn't help asking over and over again!!!

I should have stopped asking her the same question, over and over again, but I simply couldn't help my little self!!!! I was that type of lamb!

Mummy Sheep finally said, "We will be leaving in a couple of weeks." *Hooray!!!!!*

What I noticed before about Mummy Sheep was that she would sometimes look unhappy and I didn't know why. But these days she seemed a lot happier. Was it because we are going to see her flock? I really didn't know!

However, for me, I couldn't help it, I was so excited about going and was thinking about all the fun things I would be doing there. I was so looking forward to our move!

"I just want to go NOW!" I told Mummy Sheep with excitement.

"But it doesn't quite work that way, does it, Sarah?" said Mummy Sheep. She told me that I needed to be patient.

"What does it mean to be patient, Mummy Sheep?" I asked.

So, Mummy Sheep explained the meaning to me, which is: "waiting for something without being upset."

UPSET!!!???

How could I wait for something without being **UPSET!!!???**

Mummy Sheep explained to me that getting upset while I waited would make me unhappy. There was *no need* for me to be worried or unhappy. All I had to do was wait and enjoy what I had now, and those things I desired with all my heart **would truly come to pass**. I would see them.

So little lambs, if you really want something and it seems to be taking a while to come. Be encouraged:

IT WILL SOON COME TO PASS.

KEEP DREAMING ABOUT IT.

WRITE IT ON PAPER OR IN A BOOK AND LOOK AT IT EVERY DAY.

DON'T FORGET, DREAMS DO COME TRUE!!!!

Now, having decided not to get anxious about when we were actually moving, I started to help Mummy Sheep around the farm and those feelings of frustration went. I then began to think of the fun I'd have when I got to Grandma and Grandpa Sheep's farm. I was a grumpy little lamb for a while, but having changed the way I was thinking, I started to see the difference in my life. I began playing with my toys and this was great for me, it was a distraction from what I was focusing on.

We all find waiting very difficult, and sometimes we'd love to have the things we want NOW. But from now on, we are going to be lambs that won't be annoyed or anxious when waiting for something, we will be *happy while we are waiting*.

The time was drawing near for us to move, and I was extremely happy about it. I was thinking about it *a lot*, and all the fun things I would be doing. I was thinking about the boat rides I'd take, which I do like.

Now this was a new experience for me because we'd never been to Grandma and Grandpa Sheep's farm before, and we would also be living with lots of other lambs and sheep.

At the old farm we were living on our own, but at Grandma and Grandpa Sheep's farm, we were going to share living areas with other lambs and sheep. We'd be living downstairs and the other flock would be living upstairs.

I was looking forward to it and thinking it would be a party every day with so many lambs and sheep around. Although we had fresh fruits and vegetables where we were now, at Grandma and Grandpa Sheep's farm it would be different.

"Grandpa Sheep owns his own farm and we can eat as much as we want," Mummy Sheep told me!

WOW!!!! I liked the sound of that.

I do like eating some fruits and vegetables and I hope you like some of them too because they are good for you! My favourite fruits are bananas, papayas, guavas, oranges, watermelons, and mangoes, guinip, cashoo (Guyanese apple); and my favourite vegetables are pumpkins, plantains, sweet potatoes, cucumber, breadfruit, eggplants and okra (ladies' fingers).

Ask your mummy sheep or daddy sheep, grandpa and grandma sheep or your carer what vegetables and fruits they like best. Also, you can ask them to tell you what fruits and vegetables they liked eating when they were lambs. You may be surprised by their answers. You can also ask your friends, what their favourite fruits and vegetables are.

Chapter 4

Moving is always a difficult thing. There's a lot to do before and after the move, and **lots** to do on the day of the move.

Have you moved before?
How did you find it?
Was it easy?
Did you get any help?

Mummy Sheep was very good at organising things, which was helpful. I was helping a tiny bit with the packing, but it was definitely a job for grown-up sheep.

Although this was a difficult job for Mummy Sheep, she seemed strong and confident, and she knew what she was doing.

The big day had arrived, and I was over the moon with excitement. I guess that was because I was a lamb and lambs just like to play and have fun.

We lambs do not worry about work and tidying the farm. In fact, we leave that for the grown-up sheep to do.

All I was thinking about was Grandma and Grandpa Sheep's farm, and all the things I would be doing there. The journey to their farm was by a lorry, then a big boat. It was very exciting with lots to see on the way; it was fun. I had been looking forward to this day for a long time and it had finally arrived. I couldn't believe it. So, yes, I was one delighted little lamb!

After nearly six hours of packing and travelling, we were almost there. I saw the port and got really excited, only to be told that we would be getting off and getting onto a smaller ferry, for this ferry wouldn't go as far as Grandpa's farm. But I was reassured that we were closer to Grandpa Sheep's farm.

"Not long to go from there," Mummy Sheep told me with a smile.

After getting off at the port, we had to get into a smaller ferry which would then take us about half an hour to forty-five minutes to finally reach Grandpa Sheep's farm. We sat and watched as all our belongings were reloaded onto the second boat which was much smaller than the first.

As we left the port, I noticed the trees looked beautiful hanging over the side of the river. The reflection was so peaceful, and the colours looked amazing. It was a stunning picture, the different **shades** of green trees and different

types of trees. We were all getting tired; I was so pleased that this was our final journey to Grandpa and Grandma Sheep's farm.

We were almost there, feeling exhausted yet happy at the same time, I couldn't wait! It was a lovely ride, we could even hear the birds in the trees and the sound of the birds chirping beautifully; it was as if they were singing to us. It was difficult to see them in the trees; apparently, there were parrots in there as well. The water looked black but when you put it in your hand it looked clear... that was amazing. Everything smelt fresh and clean; *nothing compared to the beauty of this place in my opinion*.

"I am feeling very excited," I said to Mummy Sheep.

It wasn't long before we were there at Grandma and Grandpa Sheep's farm. With all the excitement of getting there, we were not disappointed. Mummy Sheep did a great job of explaining and describing Grandpa Sheep's farm to us, it was as she said.

As we came around the bend of the river, the farm was just in front of us. Oooh, it was a lovely feeling of joy.

"We are here! Hey!" I shouted.

I was soooooo happy, and feelings of total excitement were rising inside me. We were all very tired from all the travelling, but we lambs still wanted to go and play and explore.

It was lovely to be here. When we got to Grandpa and Grandma Sheep's farm the entire flock was out and waiting for us; it was a great welcome party.

Having greeted everyone, we were off to explore! The farm was about 10 times bigger than our old farm, there was so much space to run around. *Oh wow, soooo much to do here. It would take us a while to see everything!* So, while Daddy Sheep, Mummy Sheep and the other sheep helped to unpack, we did what lambs do best – we hopped, skipped and ran away to play and left the unpacking for the grown-ups to do.

I noticed one day that Mummy Sheep was looking happy, I could see that she was no longer sad. She was pleased to be with her mummy and daddy sheep. She was walking around with a smile on her face. Mummy Sheep was indeed thrilled to be with her flock.

It had been a long time since she'd seen her flock, and now that we were all here, she was at peace. You could see that Mummy Sheep was really at peace and very happy to be with her flock again.

It was also great for us to be able to spend that time with Grandpa and Grandma Sheep and the other sheep and lambs. I was really happy that Mummy Sheep was able to see and be with her flock, and also it was great that she had that special time with *her* mummy and daddy sheep and that was important for her.

Chapter 5

Having many grown up sheep living on the same farm was awesome. We lambs were able to play and did not have to help unpack boxes. Because there were many helping hooves around, we weren't needed at all and that gave us the time to play with the other lambs. I wasn't needed to do jobs around the farm just yet, but I knew that would change in a few weeks when we had settled down at our new farm.

It took a while to get settled to normal life at Grandma and Grandpa Sheep's farm. I didn't want to miss out on anything, so for me playing was what I had in mind before we came, and I did just that. I was pleased that Mummy Sheep allowed me to play rather than give me my little chores to do.

I did like helping Mummy Sheep tidy up the farm, and she liked my help too. But as Mummy's little helper I was given permission to play... definitely no chores for now! So, we were off to play with the animals, and run around with the other lambs, playing different games. This is what I had been thinking and dreaming about, and now we were finally here I just wanted to enjoy this beautiful farm.

We played that first night with the other lambs well into the night, which was fun. This was not something we did regularly. Mummy Sheep usually made sure we were in bed at a particular time. You know what Mummy Sheep told us all time? "Going to bed early and having a good night's sleep helps you to grow healthily." That could very well be true since I am a now a much older and much wiser sheep.

The freedom to run around with other lambs was

amazing, we were having the time of our lives. It was great having lots of playmates to play with, it was an enjoyable time.

At our old farm I used to play and talk to my imaginary friend, but now I had lambs to play with which was wonderful.

Grandma and Grandpa Sheep's farm was enormous with a massive field and plenty of creative things to do. It was a very peaceful place to be, and at the same time there was so much going on.

Despite having boats go by in the mornings from time to time, the area was still very quiet. In the evening it would be extremely calm, and I could see why Mummy Sheep liked it here. She was happy to be with her flock and I could now see why. It was a place of total peace and beauty.

One evening, after Mummy Sheep had put us to bed, we noticed something lying over the window. As I look intensely at the object, I realised that it was a snake coiled up and asleep! I couldn't believe what I was seeing, so I called out to Mummy Sheep, and she came running to us.

I pointed to the object lying on the ledge of the window. When she saw what it was, she looked a picture - her face told it all - she was horrified!

Lying over the window was a snake. I could see that Mummy Sheep was scared but what she did next made us feel very proud to have a mummy sheep like her. Slowly and quietly, Mummy Sheep went over to the window and took a closer look at the snake to see how it was lying. Then she whispered to us not to say anything or make a sound. As she moved closer, she whispered to us again... "Be quiet and don't move."

Slowly, yet swiftly, she grabbed the snake by the neck and took it outside. *Ooh, what a brave Mummy Sheep we have!*

Because of the warmth indoors, the snake came in to keep warm.

"I don't blame him," I said. "But I sure don't want to be lying next to a snake," I told Mummy Sheep.

Chapter 6

We were told some very important news, which was: Mummy Sheep was pregnant! We were going to have another little lamb in our flock. I was really happy.

"That is the best news ever," I said. "Can we have a girl lamb please?" I would love us to have a girl lamb. "Let the lamb be a girl," I prayed.

Having our own baby lamb to play with in our own flock would be wonderful. It was lovely to have lots of lambs around to play with - for it's not much fun playing on your own. But, saying that, I sometimes liked playing on my own! I guess you can have imaginary friends like I had, where I would imagine that Mummy Sheep's bed was a platform and that my cot was a boat, and that the cupboards were my shops, while talking to my imaginary friends. Playing by yourself could be fun sometimes but having lots of lambs around was wonderful.

So, the time came for our baby lamb to be born. Mummy Sheep needed to go to a special place where lambs are born. We had to wait for about three days for Mummy Sheep to come home. I did miss Mummy Sheep, but now I was so looking forward to seeing her *and* our new lamb.

There was so much excitement on the farm when we heard that Mummy Sheep and baby lamb were coming home. And guess what? It was a girl lamb!!! And just to say, we didn't have a phone back then so the only way for us to communicate was by letter or telegram, or to send a message with a friend (which was sometimes faster I must say).

"YAH!!!!!!!!!!"

They both got home safely. I was hoping the little lamb would be a girl, and so it was. Ooooh, she was an adorable and cute lamb. We checked and saw that all her limbs were in the right places, which was funny.

"At last, we have a girl lamb to play with of our own," I thought, "especially now that this sweet, cute lamb is one of us, she belongs to our flock." I was very happy that both Mummy Sheep and the baby lamb were well.

We could now say we were a flock of three lambs and a daddy and mummy sheep. Our flock was growing and that's great because having a big flock meant lots of lambs to play with. Also, I thought that a big flock was far better than a small flock, as you could do fun things together as the saying goes, 'the more the merrier.'

Unfortunately, not long after Baby Lamb was born, Daddy Sheep shared with us that we wouldn't be staying much longer at Grandpa and Grandma Sheep's farm, and that was because of our growing flock. This was sad to hear as I would miss the lambs and the sheep here. We had been having so much fun and now we had to say another goodbye.

Having a tiny lamb who had just been born, was a bonus for us. However, this was very much an issue for Mummy Sheep as she would miss her flock very much.

Mummy Sheep and Daddy Sheep had found us a

pasture that would be spacious and comfortable for us. So here we were again... moving.

Our new pasture was enormous; it had so much space that we could run, jump and skip in it. I loved it here. The only downside to moving away from Grandpa and Grandma Sheep's pasture was that we weren't able see them regularly. Nevertheless, we were enjoying our new pasture and having lots of fun.

There were horses and other animals on our new pasture, but we were not allowed to play with them because Mummy Sheep preferred us to be clean and tidy and not to get our wool messy. However, we did go out in the fields and play when the sun was out.

Visitors, from time to time, came and visited us, but it was not the same as being at Grandpa and

Grandma's farm. Although we had lots of space in which to play, I was not very happy because I missed the other lambs at Grandpa and Grandma Sheep's farm. They had an enormous pasture and we were able to go anywhere without being afraid but now, on our new farm, we weren't allowed to play freely. This was very sad for us; Mummy Sheep had to always keep an eye on us.

From time to time Grandma and Grandpa Sheep would come and visit us, which was fun, and we always looked forward to their visit. They usually brought us fresh vegetables and fruits from their farm. We were extremely happy when they came over because they always brought us goodies that we loved.

We were never happy when they left us because we had fun when they came to visit, and Mummy Sheep was always very pleased to have her mummy and daddy sheep around. Grandad was a very funny sheep and we loved him being with us.

So, we said our goodbyes to Grandma and Grandpa Sheep when they would leave us, and we looked forward to their next visit.

Chapter 7

I asked Daddy Sheep, one day, if it was possible for me to ride a horse. He said, "Yes, that'll be fine. You will need to be ready, and one day when I am home early from work and the weather is dry, you can have that riding lesson."

So, I began looking forward to riding the horse with Daddy Sheep. Every day I would be prepared and ready for that adventure of my life.

All looked well, the weather was right, and it looked like a good day for horse riding. It wasn't raining, which was brilliant. So yes, it was a perfect day for the thrill of my life.

I could see Daddy Sheep in the distance, heading

home and riding on the horse. I was getting mixed feelings about riding a horse. I started to feel nervous but happy at the same time, and Mummy Sheep reassured me that all would be well. I decided to help Mummy Sheep in the farm, for this would keep my mind off my horse-riding adventure. I didn't want to think too much about the horse-riding lesson because I was feeling nervous; I didn't want the horse to sense my fear for that wouldn't make him feel happy about me.

Soon Daddy Sheep was home, and I was in the pasture for my riding lesson. The pasture was huge, and the grass was long and soft, so if I should fall off the horse, I would be fine; I wouldn't hurt myself badly.

"I'll have a soft landing," I thought.

Now all was set, and I was ready for my first horse-riding lesson. My mind was racing... Would I like it? Only time would tell.

I had to relax, but I couldn't, I was feeling very uncomfortable and I was beginning to get scared.

Daddy Sheep got to our farm, and he was ready to give me this unique experience of riding a horse. I was a bit nervous and not sure what to expect. It looked easy and comfortable, but was it?

I was assisted onto the horse, and Daddy Sheep had a firm grip on the reigns as we walked; we were off. I was riding a horse for the first time, and ooh I was **not** enjoying it!

I didn't think I could do it much longer, I wanted to get off. I told myself that this would definitely be my last… yessss… my first *and last* horse-riding lesson!

After that experience, I concluded that horse-riding was not for everyone, especially me. However, if you should have an opportunity to ride a horse, take it. You *may* enjoy it.

Many lambs have fun riding horses, so be brave, this might be something you will really like, or you may not… As for me, I won't do it again!

Chapter 8

Sometime later... After a long day, we were all ready for a good night's rest. Everyone was in bed and we could hear noises coming from the guitar which was on top of the wardrobe. We weren't sure what exactly was causing the noise that was coming from the guitar.

Whatever was going in and out of the guitar was keeping us up, and this went on for a while. We tried to ignore it but couldn't. Then Daddy Sheep decided to investigate, and, to our amazement, in the guitar were mice - **LOADS** of them!

We started laughing, knowing that mice were playing our guitar. That was funny, so Daddy Sheep got rid of them and moved the guitar from where it was and placed it in our living area. From that day onwards, we were not disturbed again by guitar playing mice.

Chapter 9

Meanwhile, things seemed to be going fairly smoothly until Daddy Sheep and Mummy Sheep broke the news to us that we were leaving this farm.

"Moving again, why?" I asked. "Now we'll be even further away from Grandpa Sheep's farm," I said to myself.

This news was very sad to hear. I had all these questions: "When were we going to see them again? Would we come back here to live or even visit? Were we going to stay away for a long time?" I didn't know what to expect anymore, there were so many uncertain things!

It's sad to leave somewhere that you are familiar with to then live in a place that you do not know or are unfamiliar with.

So here we were again... Mummy Sheep was busy packing things in boxes and bags (with a little help from me). After days of packing and saying our goodbyes, we were ready to leave... It was a very sad day for us.

Chapter 10

Mummy and Daddy Sheep had found a farm and this one was very different to what we were used to. There were lots more, and I mean LOTS more, sheep and lambs.

Now at this new farm we could hardly see any trees. We had plenty of trees at our last farm, but our new farm was completely different.

The neighbours were lovely and very welcoming. We had so many of them around us, and they were kind and willing to help us. Whenever we needed their assistance they were there in a flash. There were quite a lot of barns around, which were big, and there were some small ones too. The farms were smaller here than at

Grandpa Sheep's farm.

Also, at the farm we were living on before, we got to play outside without any trouble but not now on our new farm. Everything had changed. This new place was called, Good Faith.

As we settled down and got to know our neighbours, things seem to be going well... until Mummy Sheep told me that I would be going to a place where I would be able to play with lots of lambs and would be taught by sheep. She said I would learn new things at this place that would help me in life, and that I would enjoy meeting and playing with some new friends.

This was too quick for me as I hadn't quite gotten used to my surroundings.

"I wanted to get to know our neighbours a bit more, play with the other animals. This is too quick!" I protested.

But Mummy Sheep wasn't having it! So, before I knew it, I was off to a place with lots of other little lambs learning to read and write and playing with other lambs.

It is very hard for a lamb to leave their barn where they feel happy and everything is familiar. I didn't like leaving our farm to be with other lambs and sheep who I didn't know, I had never done that before and being there was upsetting me.

I missed Mummy Sheep a lot when I was there. I cried and cried so much. "I want to go home, I don't want to stay here!" I cried.

After a while, I began to settle into this flock. I cried when Mummy Sheep dropped me off for a couple weeks, until I understood the routine that she dropped me off in the morning and picked me up at round 13:00 hours.

The lambs were very nice to me. They played and

shared their toys with me. The sheep were very kind also and they taught me lots of new things.

"I like it here. The lambs are lovely to me," I said to Mummy Sheep when she came to pick me up. I was very happy to see Mummy Sheep when she came pick me up, I was over the moon with excitement with this new arrangement.

I began to enjoy my time spent with this flock. Besides, they were nice to me, and now these lambs became my new friends. I began to play with them, and it wasn't scary anymore. Mind you, it was scary at first, but now it was great! I was getting comfortable with my new friends and having fun. We were together for five days, from Monday to Friday, and were at our farms on Saturdays and Sundays, where we could play with our flocks and have fun visiting our flocks in different areas. Nevertheless, I was loving it! You could see the joy on my face.

Even though it had taken me a little while to settle in with my new friends, and get used to my new routine, I really loved it there. I was getting to know them, and they were getting to know me. We were doing all sorts of lovely things together, for example, colouring pictures, which I did love very much because it brought a picture to life. I also loved drawing which I was *really* enjoying.

Also, I became interested in art and maths, but my favourite was art. I also developed a love for books and loved reading exciting stories. So, it was great fun and I was learning lots of new things.

What do you like doing at your school that is exciting? Are you totally enjoying it?

Chapter 11

As time went by, and I was getting older, I noticed that Daddy Sheep was not behaving nicely. I discovered that even though I was doing well at school and at home, Daddy Sheep expected even more from me and I mean **lots more**. So, he gave me more work to do and he would get REALLY, REALLY upset if I was not doing well.

This change in attitude I noticed in Daddy Sheep was not only towards me, but also towards Mummy Sheep. I was not happy with what I was seeing, and this was making me very unhappy. I noticed Mummy Sheep crying one day, and this bothered me.

Why was she crying? How could I help? What could I do to help her? Was there anything I could do? Why was I not able to help her?

I truly didn't like to see Mummy Sheep upset, it bothered me. Because she worked very hard on our farm with the little she had, seeing her being treated unkindly upset me.

Daddy Sheep was not very pleased when I was naughty, so I had to be good, and I mean *really good* for him. This was making us little lambs very scared of him.

"He treats us unkindly and we are beginning to dislike being with him," I told Mummy Sheep one day.

There have been times when Daddy Sheep was also mean to Mummy Sheep and that really upset me. I didn't like it when Daddy Sheep was mean to Mummy Sheep, especially when she tried to defend me.

You see, Mummy Sheep grew up with a flock that encouraged her to play and have fun as well as do her homework, but for us it was different. I would have little play but lots of studying. For a lamb, this was not good!

It was a surprise one day when Daddy Sheep told us we had to move again, and this time it was because of his work. Since we'd moved a few times in the past, I was not sure if I liked it any more. We would get settled and then we'd have to move again — I didn't think it was fun, we would miss our friends that we made.

"We'll just have to make new friends again," I told myself.

Moving was always difficult for Mummy Sheep because she was the one doing most of the work, the packing and the cleaning and the sorting out. Daddy Sheep, on the other hand, helped a bit, and I do mean 'a bit'. This was due to his work, which I think was a good thing because there were fewer problems and less fights. But, on the other hand, you do need lots of help when you are moving. So, if you are moving to another farm, try and help as much as you can. It makes a difference when we can all chip in.

We began to get excited about the move and travelling. For us lambs it looked like it was going to be fun. I remember thinking that it was fun to travel all the time. So, in anticipation I began to think about our new place and imagine that it might be good once we got there. We lambs started to look forward to the move with a bit of excitement, but it was *NOT* so for Mummy Sheep.

So here we were again, moving to another

pasture. This would definitely be different from the old farm where we lived before.

Moving day was here and there was so much to do; cleaning, packing and unpacking, and tidying up. There is a lot to do before and after a move, and Mummy Sheep had to unpack all our special things, and this can be tiring. I did help wherever I could as a lamb, and Mummy Sheep was always *grateful* for my little help.

She made it looked so easy. She went around emptying boxes and tidying up at the same time. I couldn't do it like her. She got everything done quickly as well as taking care of us. She was busy making sure our new farm looked like a home as soon as we were there. Within a few hours, our farm always looked and felt like we'd lived there for months. She placed things in their rightful place almost immediately.

It was getting late and we hadn't explored our new pasture or said hello to our new friends in the other farms. It was a pleasure to meet our new friends the next day.

Everything looked different here; the barns were closer to us. So yes, it was very different. It seemed much busier there than our last farm. There were lots of lambs and sheep around and I do mean *a lot.*

We were settling in beautifully and getting to know the other lambs in the pastures next to us. They were lovely sheep and the lambs were friendly and wanted to be our friends, which we were very pleased about. It made us feel much more at peace that the lambs were friendly towards us.

Now that we were at our new farm, we were not seeing much of Daddy Sheep, and the reason was because he was working away. He was always back every fortnight, so Mummy Sheep was always busy making sure all was well before he got home. She was that type of Mummy Sheep you see, she was always making sure everything was in order before Daddy Sheep arrived home.

Mummy Sheep was doing a great job taking care of us and making sure we were fed. She was trying her hardest to make us happy, and even though it was not easy for her, she was doing a brilliant job taking care of us.

Mummy Sheep worked really hard to make us happy which was great for us. This helped a great deal because when Daddy Sheep was around, our home was not a happy one. If you have a good daddy sheep, do say to him, "Thank you for being a good daddy sheep."

Some daddy sheep do fun things with their lambs and spend wonderful time with them. If you have a daddy sheep who spends time with you often, give him a big hug and say, thank you.

I think daddy sheep should *not* stop playing with their lambs in the pastures. They should always have those special moments with their lambs. This was very important to us lambs and we loved it.

Some daddy sheep still do fun things with their lambs and this is great. This relationship between daddy sheep and lambs is very important. It is not only good for the lambs but very good for daddy sheep as well.

If you do not have a daddy sheep around, what could you do, you may ask? I think you should not be upset or afraid or even sad because you may have another daddy sheep around who is willing to be a daddy sheep to you. He may be kind and loving and want to see you succeed. He may want you to be safe and may want to protect you at all costs. **Now that's a good daddy sheep.**

Some daddy sheep are loving and kind and maybe your daddy sheep is the opposite. Don't worry. Be strong and always remember that you are special and cuddly, and you are loved.

You are a winner!!!!!

So have a fun time in your farm and explore your farm, whether you have a daddy sheep or not.

See you soon...

THE END

Remember to look out for the other books coming soon!

About the Author

Sharda was born in the small country of Guyana which is situated in the South American continent and has a population of around 782,225 people. Guyana was once a British colony many years ago and is now the only English-speaking nation in that region.

Sharda has been living in the United Kingdom for over 20 years, she is married and has two children. She is a qualified hairdresser and has completed two years of Bible School. She loves meeting and talking with people, reading and writing, and finds that there are never enough pens and books for her. Sharda's desire to write has been in her heart for a long time, and now that desire ("DREAM") has become a reality.

Sharda's desire is to encourage children of all ages to have a DREAM and never give up on that DREAM, for they do come to pass. When someone has a dream in life, it is that dream that will keep them when things are tough, and when nothing is going the way they would like it to be, their DREAM is what will keep them going. It is that DREAM that will give them purpose and fill them with determination to see those DREAMS become something they can touch, see and smell.

Sharda heard Evangelist Jesse Duplantis at a conference in Birmingham 1997 say, *"Determination is the vehicle faith rides in."* Sharda was determined to see those DREAMS she had in her heart become a reality.

People with DREAMS are trendsetters. However long it takes and whatever you may face in this life, when your heart is set and focused, you are sure to reach your destination, accomplish your purposes and fulfil your destiny.

Sharda believes that our young people today have lost sight of their PURPOSE, they need to know that they are born for a PURPOSE. If you know that you are hurting or stopping someone from reaching their full potential in life, you are also stopping yourself from reaching your destiny. She believes that young people of today should stay focused on those DREAMS they have and NOT lose sight of them. Sharda's goal is to encourage our young people to DREAM and to DREAM BIG, for DREAMS do come true. She can testify to that!

Printed in Poland
by Amazon Fulfillment
Poland Sp. z o.o., Wrocław